P9-DGW-638

BOOKS BY BETTY JEAN LIFTON

The Cock and the Ghost Cat
The Dwarf Pine Tree
Good Night, Orange Monster
Jaguar, My Twin
The Mud Snail Son
The One-Legged Ghost
Return to Hiroshima
Children of Vietnam
(by Betty Jean Lifton and Thomas C. Fox)

JAGUAR,

MY TWIN

Betty Jean Lifton

JAGUAR,
My Twin

ILLUSTRATED BY

Ann Leggett

Atheneum · 1976 · New York

Library of Congress Cataloging in Publication Data

Lifton, Betty Jean. Jaguar, my twin.

SUMMARY: A descendant of the Mayas, Shun becomes ill
when his twin soul, a young jaguar,
is released from the supernatural corral.
I. Leggett, Ann. II. Title.
PZ7.L6225Jag [Fic] 76–4475
ISBN 0–689–30526–5

Published simultaneously in Canada by
McClelland & Stewart, Ltd.
Manufactured in the United States of America
Halliday Lithograph Corporation
West Hanover, Massachusetts
Designed by Mary M. Ahern
First Edition

FOR

Karen, Ken, Dimitri, Noah

AND

All the Dreamers of the Sna

Acknowledgements

With special thanks to Robert Laughlin who sees and dreams well; to Robert Wasserstrom who shared his knowledge and time; to Evon Z. Vogt for writing his book *Zinacantan: A Maya Community in the Highlands of Chiapas* and setting up the Harvard Chiapas Project; and to Robert Jay Lifton, Florence and Richard Falk and Patricia McCarthy for sharing it all.

Contents

Contents

Part 1

THE
DREAM

Day
of the
Dream

Shun can think of nothing but the dream he has just had. It is hard for him to concentrate on selling his flowers on that remote mountain road in southeast Mexico, because his mind keeps returning to the night before when his soul was out visiting. For when you dream, your soul goes visiting—has adventures of its own. At least that's what Shun's Indian tribe believes.

Shun could not have said just what a soul is—although he knows that everyone and everything has one: even his house and the corn on which his people depend for their livelihood. During the day the soul is in the back of your head or in your heart, but when darkness falls, it might sit on the tip of your nose or

3

go wandering about in your dreams.

The night before, Shun's soul had taken its most important journey. It has been hard for him to return to his waking state and put his mind on selling flowers. Indeed, he has already let many cars pass by before he even heard their motors. As a result he hasn't sold a single bunch, and the gladiolus and daisy blossoms are beginning to wilt in the mid-morning sun.

Now he decides to shut the dream from his thoughts until he can return home for lunch to tell his mother. And so when he hears the next motor, even before it has turned the curve on the road, he springs forward, arm outstretched, waiting.

He watches as the large foreign car speeds toward him. For a moment he is sure its motor is slowing down, as if the people inside are considering the possibility of stopping. Through the open window he sees a boy about ten, his own age, in the back seat. He has blond hair and eyes as pale as the sky at dawn, unlike his own which are as dark as the night sky.

The boy waves at him, but the car presses on up

the road to the large market town of San Cristobal.

Shun does not wave back. This road, the Pan American Highway, has just been finished and he is not used to seeing tourists. He still does not feel relaxed enough to do more than sell them the flowers he grows in the small plot behind his house in the valley below.

His people, the Zinacantecs, known as the proud and energetic People of the Bat, do not mix unnecessarily with the outside world.

Now Shun sits down on the roadside next to his flowers. He watches as open trucks take some of his tribesmen down to the hot lowlands to rented cornfields, and as buses carry others up toward the San Cristobal market. He watches them arriving and leaving until his head is reeling, as if his people, these trucks and buses, this road, and even the foreign boy in that car that didn't stop, are all a dream.

His dream.

When the sun is directly overhead, he can wait no longer. He hurries down the steep embankment to his house nestled close to the others in the mist-filled valley. His mother was too busy that morning grinding corn dough and making tortilla pancakes for his father's breakfast to hear his dream, but she will have more time now.

"Are you there?" he calls at the gate. It is his customary greeting, although he knows that by now she is surely back from washing their clothes at the water hole.

"Here I am," replies his mother from inside, as she always does.

He goes over to the cooking fire where she sits with his baby sister Maruch strapped on her back. Katal, his six-year-old sister, is playing with bottle caps on the earth floor at her side.

The baby reaches out a hand to Shun for the usual peso to play with, and he is sorry he does not have one to give her. He scoops up one of the bottle caps at his feet and offers it instead. He is careful not to get her too excited, for a baby's soul is not as firmly attached to the body as it will be later, and there is the danger at all times of losing it.

More than once Shun has seen his mother brush off the spot where she was sitting with the baby in order to gather back any of the thirteen parts of its soul that may have fallen by chance.

Now Shun lifts Maruch from his mother's back and rocks her gently. She is quite content and lays back passively, looking into his eyes as he settles himself on a small stool by the fire. Katal nestles against his knee to hear what news he might have brought from the road. She is almost a miniature of her mother in her white blouse and long blue skirt, her hair also parted in the middle with two long braids, her feet bare.

"I had a dream last night," Shun announces to them all.

His mother looks up from the large round squash she is about to cut with a machete.

"Tell us," she urges eagerly.

For she knows that the world of dreams and the waking world on the earth's surface are one and the same thing—except that what happens to you when you sleep is more important than anything that happens in your waking state. A good dream can hold the key to your fortunes, yes, just as a bad one can foretell a disaster.

"Tell us, tell us!" repeats Katal, pulling at the red

tassel on the stole he always wears over his tunic.

"Listen," says Shun. "It seems that I was cutting a trail through the forest with my machete when suddenly there was a clearing, and I saw a mountain just ahead to the east."

His mother interrupts, "A mountain, yes? What shape was it?"

"It was tall, with many peaks that seemed to be pointing to the heavens."

"Could you see into the mountain?" his mother asks, trying to contain her excitement.

"No, even as I glimpsed it, it became covered with clouds."

Shun's mother smiles mysteriously.

"Your time is getting close," she says. And she scoops up some beans into a bowl and hands it to him.

Shun knows, without her saying more, what she means. For he has dreamed of Senior Great Mountain where, it is said, the ancestral gods live. It is there that they sit in their great banquet hall eating and drinking the offerings that are sent to them, granting favors to those who lead virtuous lives or punishing those who break the social codes.

However, most important, it is on that mountain that the gods keep the Supernatural Corral, which is filled with the ten thousand animals who are the twin souls of each one of his people.

Before Shun was born, his twin soul was placed in one of the animals of the corral. But he does not know which one. His animal spirit companion might be a jaguar, an ocelot, a coyote or maybe one of the smaller creatures like a racoon, an anteater, an opossum, or even a hawk or an owl. After the age of seven, if one is lucky, one might see his twin spirit in a dream, yes.

And now that Shun has dreamed of the sacred mountain where the Supernatural Corral is kept, he might soon have that dream. That's what his mother meant when she said his time was coming close, even though she knew as well as he did that some people never in their whole lives dream of the mountain, let alone the corral inside.

Shun hopes that his animal spirit companion is a jaguar, for this is the most beautiful of the beasts, worshipped by his Mayan ancestors because of its power and cunning.

But he knows that whatever animal it is, he has to be on guard at all times, for anything that happens to him will happen to his twin spirit. And likewise, anything that happens to his twin on Senior Great Mountain, such as getting thrown out of the corral for displeasing the gods or being shot by one of the many hunters who lie in wait for just such hapless animals, will cause a terrible fate to fall on him down on the earth's surface.

Shun has learned early that it is important to do things the right way, yes—keep your clothes and body clean, work hard in the fields, and lead a blameless life—so that the gods will take good care of your animal spirit companion up there on the mountain. And he hopes that his animal understands that it must also live in harmony with the others, not fight with any of them, and stay safely within the corral.

"Do you think I'll dream of my animal twin companion soon?" he asks his mother.

"I don't know," she says thoughtfully. "It may be tonight, next month, next year—or never."

Then seeing his disappointed face, she adds, "But I think it will probably be soon, yes."

Romin

"Shun, I'm over here!"

It is Romin, Shun's best friend, up on the road. Just a year ago they used to wander idly around the village catching birds with their slingshots, teasing the girls tending sheep, and spinning tops.

But now the two of them are busy growing flowers in their gardens and selling them on the highway. They are hovering between the pleasures of boyhood and the responsibilities of men, which will soon be thrust upon them. Romin's older brother is already working in the fields in the lowlands with his father and is engaged to be married.

Shun has missed Romin in the morning and is surprised to see him now.

"Where were you?" he calls with a wave, after he catches his breath from the steep climb up from the valley.

Romin waits until Shun has joined him to answer. "I had to help my mother herd the sheep."

Shun winces. He has not done that for some time —considers himself much too old now. Herding sheep is a girl's job, like washing clothes, weaving and cooking.

"She's feeling weak these days," explains Romin. "If she's not better by tomorrow, Father says he is going to have a shaman find out if someone has put black magic on her."

Shun's heart races a little. Everyone dreads getting sick because no one knows if it is something caused by nature or by an enemy who has sent an illness on the wind to you.

"I'm sure she'll be all right," he reassures Romin, although he knows that no one can ever be sure. To cheer his friend up now, he tells him his dream, word by word, as he had told his mother.

"Are you sure you couldn't see into the mountain, just a little?" Romin presses him.

"I really tried," says Shun. "But the clouds kept moving in."

"My father says that in the old days everyone

could see into the mountain," says Romin. "But now only the shamans can. Don't you wish we had lived in those ancient days?"

"But we did," replies Shun.

He is thinking of what his father told him when his baby brother died a few years before—that the soul flies around like a fly for as many days as the body lived on earth. And then it is reborn in the opposite sex into the tribe.

"Well, what good does it do us, if we don't remember," grunts Romin. He looks at Shun playfully. "If you had a choice, what animal would you choose for a twin?"

"A jaguar, of course. What else?"

"I might take a weasel."

They both laugh at the thought of Romin as a weasel.

"Why?"

"He's clever and quick and can get into small places," replies Romin with a grin. He was always a tease.

"How about a coyote?" says Shun. "My mother says thin people are usually coyotes."

"I'm not that thin!" roars Romin.

And then the two friends are so busy giggling over all the possible animals who might be their twin spirits, that many cars pass by before they remember the business at hand—selling flowers.

Shun's Father

That night as Shun's family is sitting around the fire where they always gather for warmth as well as food, there is no time to talk of Shun's dream. Shun's father has announced on entering their one-room house that he has something to tell them. Everyone is nervously waiting for his piece of news.

Shun's father is always full of new ideas, which he usually carries through. Once, in just such a voice as he is using tonight, he announced he had decided to replace their thatch roof with tile. And before Shun's mother could find enough arguments against this— like tile holds in the smoke from the cooking fire and is expensive—his father had done it.

"In the long run, tile will need less repairs than thatch," he had said decisively, closing the subject. And theirs was the first village house to have it.

For although Shun's father respects the codes of the ancestors, he does not seem to fear making changes as do many of his tribesmen. He is one of the leaders in the hamlet, taking an active part in the various fiestas that mark the seasons, and few people can speak against him.

But some do.

"What has happened?" Shun's mother asks her

husband nervously, as she kneels in her usual way to serve him his tortillas and beans. She will eat later when he is done.

"It is not what *has* happened, but what *will* happen," says her husband, scooping up the beans with a piece of tortilla.

"Yes?"

They are all waiting.

"I have heard," he continues, "that the government is offering to place poles in the hamlets of any tribe that wants electricity."

He looks around at their faces, upon which the flickering fire is casting its dim glow.

"With electric lights we'll be able to see each other more clearly," he points out. And then he adds with a chuckle: "Though we may look better in the dark."

But Shun and his mother do not respond to his joke.

They are remembering the last time the government made an offer—water pipes. His father had been just as enthusiastic about having water faucets, but the issue had divided the tribesmen into two factions. One, led by their grumpy neighbor, Manvel, had been violently opposed to it.

"The gods have given us sacred water holes and lakes," Manvel had argued. "We should not try to improve upon their gifts."

But Shun's father was a persuasive speaker, with a fast way of turning a phrase.

"The gods may be sending water to us now in this new form to ease our lives," he had replied. "One must be careful not to refuse a gift from the gods."

No one could think of an answer to that. The result was that most of the men had voted for the water pipes. Three water faucets now sat next to the Mexican school, which had been put in by the government a few years before, also by his urging.

"At least electricity will be of more value to the hamlet than those water faucets are," Shun's father is saying now with a grin.

This time he does get a laugh from his wife and son. For everyone knows that no one lives close enough to the Mexican school to use the water from the pipes. Very few children have enough time or interest to attend classes, let alone bring water home, so busy are they helping their parents with chores.

And so the women have continued to fill their huge jugs at the water holes, which they secretly prefer anyway, since it gives them time to meet and gossip with each other.

The rusty water faucets are by now a family joke.

But it is no joke that Manvel and his kinfolk have not spoken to Shun's family since then. There is an uneasy tension between the two houses, separated only by a small cornfield and a wooden fence.

Should one of Shun's mother's chickens wander into the other yard, it will never return. This sometimes worries his mother, because no one wants an enemy who might cause the wind to carry an illness to you. They have all stayed well until now, but what if this new issue over electricity makes Manvel even angrier?

Shun's mother does not want to take a chance.

"Well, we have managed without electric lights until now," she says. "And it will probably be too expensive to use, won't it?"

"Not if we hang just one bulb from the center post," her husband replies.

"But we go to bed shortly after nightfall," she continues. "The fire throws enough light until then."

Shun's father is losing his good mood. "Shun must study Spanish. Our Indian language will not be enough for him."

"It's been enough for you," retorts his wife. "You've managed everything with nothing but Tzotzil."

"And I've had to depend on government interpreters to get what I wanted for the hamlet," he replies. "My son should go beyond me. With Spanish he can hold high offices in the tribe."

He pauses and runs his fingers affectionately over Katal's face as she peers anxiously up at him. She is frightened by his tone of voice. "And I want my little girl to study hard, too," he adds more softly, pulling at her pigtail.

"I will need Katal to help me weave and cook," argues his wife. "If she reads at night, she'll be too tired the next day. That goes for Shun, too, in the fields."

"The children can work and study, *both*," her husband says at last in that firm voice that means the subject is closed.

Shun has kept silent while his parents were quarreling, but now he speaks up.

"I wonder what Manvel will say when he hears about the government's offer."

His father smiles slyly. "He will probably say, 'Look here, fellow villagers, this electricity is some trick to control us.' "

He imitates Manvel's squeaky voice so well that even Shun's mother has to laugh. Katal and Shun let out whoops of joy and roll with mirth on the floor. One would think they were all drinking *posh,* the homemade rum drink distilled from sugar and water that all Zinacantecs love.

"Quiet down," says Shun's father, looking outside through the door. "Manvel may hear us and prepare his arguments in advance."

But this only encourages more peals of laughter. The giddy mood stays with them until the fire goes down, and it is almost time to climb onto their platform beds and cover themselves with blankets, for in the highlands the temperature drops at night, and the cold seeps through your bones.

Creatures
of the
Night

There is no bathroom or even an outhouse in Shun's village. One uses the fields. Now as Shun makes his way with a sputtering kerosene lantern into the darkness beyond his house, he thinks how good it will be to have electricity shining from the doorway.

Although he would never admit it, Shun is always a little afraid when he comes out here alone. Once he was sure he saw a wild goat go by, and everyone knows that a goat seen at night is really a witch in disguise.

Another time he thought he saw little dark men with winged feet who would have carried him away to their cave if he hadn't rushed back into the house just in time.

And there was one particularly black, starless night when he was sure he saw the Earth Lord, who owns the land and causes lightning and earthquakes, ride by on his deer. Yes, he saw him, using iguanas for blinders over the deer's eyes and a snake for a whip. One is supposed to be grateful to the Earth Lord for trees to build houses, mud for its walls, and rain for the crops, but still one does not want to meet him on a dark road at night. There are stories that when he needs workers, he captures anyone he finds and makes them labor in his underground kingdom until the iron shoes he gives them wear out. And iron doesn't wear out very quickly.

"When there is electricity, I won't have to be afraid of the Earth Lord," Shun tells himself. "Or of balls of fire or demons. Evil creatures don't like the light."

And then relieved in more ways than one, he hurries back into the house and into bed.

"But what if Manvel really does get angry?" he wonders as he falls into a dreamless sleep.

The
Meeting

The cocks crow all night, and the dogs bark, "*Vom, vom, vom,*" but finally it is dawn. The villagers are astir even earlier than usual so that the men can do their chores before attending the hamlet meeting on whether or not to have electricity.

Shun has decided not to sell flowers on the road today, but to go with his father.

As soon as they hear the blast of the horn summoning them to the town meeting hall, men and boys pour out of all the houses onto the one dirt path that circles the hamlet.

"Go and come back," Shun's mother says as they leave to join the others.

"I am going," is his father's customary reply. He adds nothing else.

By the time they reach the low-slung wooden hut

that serves as the town hall, there is a large crowd milling about in front. Soon it will be too hot to go inside, and so they assemble on the covered patio. The elders sit on a long bench, while the younger men group around them, and boys like Shun watch on the edges.

The men don't seem to mind standing as they attend such sessions. Some of them are busy plaiting palm fiber into new straw hats, which they will trim with pink and purple ribbons streaming down their backs like the long bird feathers their Mayan ancestors once wore.

A stranger in the hamlet would have trouble knowing who were the wealthy among the men, for, except on festival days, they always dress exactly alike: red striped tunics that their women had woven, with black and white checked stoles over them, and either handmade short white pants or store-bought long trousers, which fall over their open leather sandals.

They wear these colorful garments proudly from the time they are boys like Shun, for they are the uniform of the tribe.

When the meeting starts, Shun's father is standing

with his faction, Manvel with his. Shun and Romin creep up front so that they will not miss anything being said.

They can see Manvel's gloomy expression as he whispers with his friends. The boys have long ago nicknamed him Chicken Face because his nose is long and thin like a beak, and his mouth sets tightly pursed as if he is constantly clucking in disapproval of the things he sees about him.

Chicken Face's young son, nicknamed Spindly Legs, is there too, and sticks out his tongue at them as their eyes meet in the crowd. His cousin, whom they call Flapping Clothes, because his tunic is always too loose, shakes his fist.

The struggle is on.

Manvel Chicken Face has no sooner called for quiet than he begins a long speech. His words are as sharp as his features as he describes the disasters that electricity will bring. It sounds as if he is expecting the end of the world.

"Look here, fellow villagers, about this electricity. What do you think? This electricity, it's a present the government says. But the Mexicans are tricky, you know. They want to control us. What good would it do them to make us Indians such a present? Think about it . . . the wires, the poles . . . they're not cheap. Who knows what they want? Who knows why they want us dumb Indians to have light!"

Everyone laughs nervously at this.

Manvel is encouraged. His voice becomes louder. "Look here, fellow villagers. We don't know what they want. But the electricity . . . do you know what electricity is? Electricity is just like lightning in heaven. Who knows how they make it run along a wire. But think it over, fellow villagers. Why do they want lightning to run along wires into our houses?"

Now everyone is looking very alarmed, just as Manvel hoped they would be.

"Haven't you seen a broken wire?" he continues. "Little bits of lightning coming out the ends of a broken wire, like sparks of our fires. And if you touch it, it burns. It really hurts. It could kill us!"

The Indians are muttering to each other now. Almost angrily.

"Maybe that's what they want, that tricky government!" Manvel's brother-in-law calls out. "They want to deceive us, perhaps, and kill us and burn our houses down and take our land!"

Shun's father has been leaning casually against the column supporting the patio roof. Now he straightens out to give an answer to Manvel Chicken Face's argument.

"Well, we have heard what Manvel has to say," he cries out. "But what if the Mexicans aren't trying to trick us? What if they are telling the truth when they say that they only want to do us a favor? Electricity would be useful to us. We could see well after the sun goes down. We could walk on the paths without stumbling. The women could weave at night."

"They could make us some extra clothes!" someone shouts out with a laugh.

Shun's father smiles, but he continues seriously. "We'd be fools to refuse such a gift, fellow villagers. And light for our houses would not cost too much. It would be cheaper than candles and easier than making our pitch-pine torches."

"It costs five hundred pesos to install light in each house!" counters Manvel's brother-in-law.

"Yes, but you only have to pay that once," Shun's

father replies. "And if you don't want to pay it, you don't have to have light in your house. For myself, I want light."

"What are you, afraid of the dark?" one of Manvel's friends shrieks. "Afraid to go into the corn fields at night all by yourself?"

Everyone around him snickers.

"I am not afraid of a gift that will make our lives easier," Shun's father retorts.

The village elders are now taking swigs of rum *posh* as if to help them consider this weighty problem. Soon the bottle is being passed around from one man to the next, as it always is when a group assembles. It serves to tie them together in unity even though their words may be pulling them apart.

"I hope the *posh* puts Manvel Chicken Face into a better mood," Romin whispers to Shun.

Now Manvel speaks up again.

"Listen, fellow villagers, electricity is not something to mess around with. It is like the lightning from heaven. Holy earth, holy heaven, that lightning belongs to the Earth Lord, not to us people. Who knows whether it would just stay in the wires . . . it might get out at night, just a little bit, if the light bulb isn't screwed in tight. It might get into our blood, our flesh. Think about it. Perhaps the Mexicans have sold our souls to the Earth Lord so they can make us do what they want with their horrible electricity crawling through our bodies like worms!"

Many of the Zinacantecs groan at the very thought. A few actually shudder.

Manvel feels that he is winning the argument. "What will the ancestors say?" he adds now. "Will they be pleased if we just allow ourselves to be hoodwinked like this? If we simply let ourselves be taken over? Remember the gods can see without electric light."

Now there are mutterings in favor of Manvel's side, not only from his relatives and friends, but from some of the men who have not previously taken sides. And the bottle seems to be going around even more quickly than it can be refilled.

However, Shun's father has an answer.

"We must not compare ourselves to the gods," he says quietly.

There is a hushed silence as everyone worries

about the possibility of offending the gods.

"But, fellow villagers, since we cannot see into things without help, the gods would wish us to improve our sight as much as we can. Just think, we can turn night into day as we pray to them."

His friends shout out in approval. Manvel's group keeps silent now.

How can the issue be decided? Who can tell them what to do? Only the old gods.

"I have a plan," says one of the village elders, who only a moment before looked as if he had been dozing. "Tonight the two of you"—and he nods at Manvel and Shun's father—"will dream. The gods will send us their answer through your dreams. And then when we hear, we will know what to do."

Everyone agrees that this is a very sensible plan— especially since it is time for lunch. They will reassemble the next morning to hear the two dreams. And then they will decide. They are relieved to go back to their ordinary work in the cornfields until then. They are, after all, only mortal.

Shun gets back to his house before his father, who

stays behind to get signatures from those who want electricity. Shun's mother is sitting by the fire making tortillas for lunch. Her two braids fall limply to her shoulders, which seem to sag under her white blouse. She looks worried and sad.

"Many of the tribe agreed with Father," he reports, trying to reassure her as he takes one of the hot tortillas from the basket by her side.

"He will only make more enemies from all this," she replies dully. "I fear something terrible is going to happen."

Shun knows what she is thinking. If Manvel Chicken Face becomes angry enough, he will ask one of the bad shamans outside the village to send an evil wind to his father or to sell his soul to the Earth Lord, who will make him work underground. Or he might persuade the gods to let his animal spirit companion out of the Supernatural Corral. A true enemy will stop at nothing to get even with you.

But still, Shun reminds himself, Manvel did not cause any trouble after he lost the water pipes decision.

"Just think," he says, trying to cheer his mother,

"when I learn to read and write, I can teach you and Katal. You used to say you wished you knew how."

Katal jumps up and down excitedly at the idea.

His mother smiles, but still she looks sad.

In truth, Shun's mother, for all her knowledge of dreams, as well as the traditions of her people, is a simple woman who never had a chance to go to school. Her whole life on earth's surface has been much the same: first helping her mother with household chores as a girl, and then raising babies and performing the same chores for her own family when she was grown.

But she has a special energy and quick intelligence that once attracted Shun's father when he first noticed her at a fiesta. He has never regretted the large amounts of fruit, rum, chocolate, corn, brown sugar, beans and tortillas that he had to pay her father as a bride's price. Until now he has respected her worries whenever she felt he was moving too quickly for the rest of the tribe.

Now as he enters the house, Shun's father notices his wife's worried expression.

"I collected a list of sixty names from those who

are with me so far," he says, after he has rinsed his mouth with water from the gourd she hands him.

Then he sits silently through the meal, perhaps thinking of the other men he must yet persuade. As he gets up to go to the fields, he says only, "I must be sure to dream well tonight."

And Shun quips: "Maybe Manvel will dream that the gods *want* electricity after all."

This breaks the tension, and his father's sense of humor returns.

"And I will dream they do *not* want electricity," he roars.

Shun's mother laughs so hard she has to cover her mouth with one hand and pat the baby, who is bobbing on her back, with the other.

But that night as they lay down on their straw mats, they cannot help but wonder where their souls will go visiting, and what dreams they will remember in the morning.

"It is said that what you dream in the middle of the night never comes true," Shun's mother warns in the darkness. "Try to dream just before dawn."

Part 2

BLACK
MAGIC

Shun's Second Dream

That night Shun is careful not to sleep face down, for his mother has always warned him he would be looking into his grave. Instead he sleeps on his back because he knows he is most likely to dream in that position.

And just before dawn he has the dream he has been waiting for.

He is walking along the road to Senior Great Mountain. The fog begins to lift as he comes closer. He can see now the tall outline of its peak against the sky and even some of the pine and oak trees along its base.

At the foot of the trail he comes to a large cross. It is said to be the doorway of the ancestral gods. It marks the entry to their world from the earth's surface. Kneeling, he lights candles and incense, thanking them for their kindness. Then he begins to climb.

He is walking with sure feet as if he knows just where he is going. He can hear the monkeys chattering overhead in the palm trees, discussing him. A boa slithers across his path; it stops for a moment, lifts its head in greeting and then disappears into the thicket. Brightly plumed birds sing out into the sky, announcing his arrival.

At the top of the trail there is a large clearing in the forest through which he sees the great house where the gods dwell. Next to it are the fields where they farm. For the ancestors live and work there on the mountain just as their mortal descendants do below, yes. And they set an example by their industry and kindness to each other of how their people should behave.

Just beyond the fields Shun can see the rows of pens in the Supernatural Corral where the ten thousand twin souls of his tribesmen live, an animal soul for each man, woman and child. He even sees the huge cages for the hawks and owls and other birds.

He can see the outlines of the assistants of the gods who water and feed the animal spirit companions each day. They are moving in and out of the pens now, brushing them, embracing them and checking that they are safe and content. He is careful to walk softly lest they notice him.

He begins walking toward the Supernatural Corral. He can see the individual stalls clearly now: the large ones for the bigger animals and the smaller ones for the squirrels, raccoons and weasels. But his legs carry him past the little enclosures, right up to the largest stalls of all—the ones in which the jaguars are kept.

He stops at one of them and looks through the slats of the fence. He sees a young jaguar, about his own age, sitting with its mother. How beautiful he is with his lean body and delicately spotted coat. His keen yellow eyes look right into Shun's. In that moment they know each other.

The jaguar mother's body tenses, and a low growl forms in her throat. But the young jaguar leaps up joyfully and rushes over to the fence. He puts his soft muzzle against it and licks Shun's hand through the slats. Then he rubs his head and ears along the fence, allowing Shun to pet him.

Shun gazes on his jaguar's sleek body. His noble head is crowned with tiny black rosebuds. His mighty tail sweeps back and forth majestically. He is splendid. Shun's Mayan ancestors were right in worshipping the jaguars as gods, yes. There is something magical about them that raises them above all other animals.

"Little jaguar, you are my twin spirit," Shun whispers. He opens the gate and hugs the jaguar. "We will go through life together—you up here in the Supernatural Corral and me on the earth's surface. But we will visit with each other often like this in dreams, won't we?"

And the jaguar, as if he knows what Shun is saying, nods its head and gives a deep rumbling purr in agreement.

Again they look into each other's eyes. Each sees himself in the other's form: each sees that other part that is always missing when they are not together.

"I will be back in another dream," Shun promises the jaguar. "It is up to the gods when my soul can come visiting again. But perhaps they will favor us by making it soon."

Then so that he will not disturb the gods or anger them by remaining too long, he closes the gate and walks away from the corral and on down the mountain trail toward his hamlet. For a moment he pauses, as if he would turn back. He has forgotten to tell his animal twin something. He wanted to warn him to be careful always to stay well within the safety of the corral where the gods will protect him.

But it is becoming dark on the path as the trees form a tunnel with their branches. Fog is beginning to move in and with it a damp chill that penetrates to his bones. He begins running toward his home, tripping over tree roots and dead branches, suddenly afraid, as if something or someone were pursuing him in that unfamiliar place.

Shun is still breathless when he wakes. He is almost choking. He realizes it is the smoke from the fire his mother is fanning to cook the morning breakfast.

He opens his eyes and watches as she gently blows the smoldering embers in the hearth into a new flame. Now he hears the comforting sound of her grinding the corn on the stone *metate* so that it will be soft enough to make tortillas. And then the friendly *pat pat* of her hands as she kneads the corn dough into a round pancake that she will put on a pan over the fire, where it will gradually take the shape of a delicious tortilla.

He wants to jump up and tell her his dream. But then he thinks better of it. He has heard it is wise not to tell anyone who your animal spirit companion is, for the enemy might overhear you and have a witch cast a spell on it. And should anything happen to your twin, you would suffer the same fate.

The thought of anything happening to his dear jaguar brings tears to his eyes, which he brushes away quickly for fear someone will see.

No, it is better to remain silent, for the protection of both his jaguar and himself. Someday when he and his parents are alone in the open fields, and he is sure no one else is around, he will tell them.

Now Shun's father is waking too, and his sister and the baby are beginning to stir.

"Did you have the dream?" Katal calls out to their father almost before she has opened her eyes.

"Tell us," says his mother, kneeling on the earth floor as she nurses the baby. "Did you dream?"

Shun's father sits on his low stool by the fire eating the freshly baked tortillas and drinking coffee from a tin mug.

"Yes, I had a dream," he replies. "But I shall wait to tell it at the meeting."

He too wants to hold close to his dream to keep it

safe. For although their house has no windows under which an enemy could spy, he knows sound can travel through an open door.

His family understands and finishes breakfast in silence.

The
Decision

On the road to the hamlet center Shun notices that Manvel Chicken Face's lips are pursed even tighter than usual. His son, Spindley Legs, sticks out his tongue again.

"Maybe Chicken Face didn't dream last night," Shun whispers to Romin who had come by the house to accompany him to the meeting.

"If he didn't, he'll make one up," says Romin. "I don't trust him."

Everyone arrives at town hall promptly this morning, eager to hear the two dreams. Shun and Romin push their way through the crowd, which is even larger than last time, so that they can hear too.

"Listen, fellow villagers, I had a dream," Manvel announces fiercely.

Immediately there is a hushed silence so still that

one can hear the bleating of the sheep in the nearby field, and the squeal of a pig who does not like the way he is tied to his house fence.

"I dreamed, fellow villagers, that the Earth Lord was angry with us for wanting electricity from the government. Yes, angry. He caused great earthquakes to shake our land and floods to destroy our homes."

Manvel pauses to wait for the expected gasp of horror from the assembled group.

"Earthquakes and floods, fellow villagers, you know what that means. Think of it. The gods are telling us that nothing will survive if we have electricity—not our hamlet, our homes, our families, our fields."

Everyone begins talking at once when he is finished. It seems that no one can argue with Manvel's interpretation.

Except Shun's father.

Now his voice can be heard ringing out over the others.

"I had a dream too, fellow villagers," he announces loudly.

Again there is complete silence. This time even the pig stops squealing, as if to listen.

"I, too, dreamed there was a flood," he continues, "but just before it reached our village I saw a man in a boat dive into the water. Perhaps it was the Earth Lord himself. He talked to a serpent on the bottom who was blocking up the water. The serpent agreed to leave, and a huge multicolored butterfly flew up from the flood into the air. The sun came out, the water disappeared and bright rays of gold spread through the sky."

No one speaks when he is through. Everyone is picturing the butterfly that is a symbol of good luck rising into the bright sky.

"I tell you, fellow villagers, that the Earth Lord and the gods favor our having electricity," Shun's father cries out. "They sent the great butterfly to tell us so. They spread the bright rays across the sky. They favor electricity. I ask, fellow villagers, do you?"

The rum bottle is being passed around while everyone considers this. And when the bottle is empty, its spirits seem to have lifted the spirits of the group.

"Yes, I'm in favor!" calls one.

"Light should come!" calls another.

"Electricity will be a help!" calls still another.

"Those who don't want it, don't have to share the cost," calls Romin's father. "But they should not spoil the chance for the rest of us."

A current of approval goes through the crowd at this last statement, like a bolt of the very electricity they are arguing about.

A vote is called and counted. Almost all of the tribesmen are in favor of accepting the government's offer. Only a few, Manvel and his clan, are opposed. Shun's father's side has won.

It is agreed that he and a few others will go into San Cristobal the very next week to discuss the details with the proper officials.

The bottle of rum goes around one last time to seal this agreement. It is also to bind those who lost into a bond of friendship. Everyone is so excited that no one notices that Manvel only pretends to put his lips to the bottle. He passes it on untouched.

Spindley Legs and young Flapping Clothes slink away, unable to face the teasing they may get from Shun and Romin.

Shun's father and his friends are so excited that instead of going to their fields, they all go back to Shun's house to celebrate their victory. There for the rest of the day and far into the night they sit drinking rum, joking and laughing.

Shun serves them the rum in tiny shot glasses that they pass around the group. The eldest drinks and toasts first, and the others follow in the same manner with their own toasts.

No sooner has the shot glass made its way around the group, than Shun has to begin from the beginning with a new round.

"Here's to electricity!" says one toaster.

"Here's to the wires and the poles!" says another.

"Here's to Shun and his father!" says a third.

And so it goes until everyone staggers out the door to their own homes. A few of them just collapse right there on the floor by the stools where they have been sitting and have to spend the night.

Shun helps his father into his bed. And because he has also had too many sips of rum, he falls into a deep sleep as soon as he reaches his own reed mat.

The Goat's Cave

Shun's father was to wish he had not drunk and slept so heavily that night. He might then have seen a night-flying moth over his roof, which would have warned him that someone wished him evil.

It was a moonless evening. Heavy clouds were gathering overhead, although the rainy season was not due for some weeks. It was the kind of night when witches roll over three times on the ground to turn into goats; when birds of ill omen shriek curses from the trees; when small black creatures with winged feet hide in the fields and grapple with unsuspecting victims.

It was the kind of night to be safely inside your home.

The Goat's Cave

When most of the hearth fires had been put out, a darting form could be seen on the path that led out of the hamlet into the limestone hills just beyond. It came from the direction of Manvel's house and moved rapidly up the steep clay trail of the farthest hill. It *was* Manvel, his face covered with his stole. He breathed heavily, squatting occasionally to rest.

Finally he took a winding side trail and ended up at the mouth of the cave known to belong to the most fearsome shaman in the area: a witch doctor who dealt only in sickness and death.

This shaman, whose spirit was as deformed as his twisted body, had mastered the art of black magic. He knew how to take part or all of a person's soul.

The adults of Shun's tribe called him "the thrower of illness." But the children had secretly nicknamed him Goat. They fled in terror the few times they encountered him in the hills, where he went to gather herbs and wild roots for his deadly medicines.

It was to Goat's cave that Manvel had made his way.

"Are you there?" he hissed outside the door as softly as he could. He was afraid the wind might carry his voice right back to his hamlet and everyone would know what he was up to. He could be imprisoned and sentenced to hard labor if he were caught in such a place.

"I am here," came a sharp voice from within.

Manvel entered the cave a little fearfully. He had never been here before.

"What is your business with me?" asked Goat, putting a few pieces of wood on the fire for his caller. No one sought him out unless he had some terrible plan in his heart.

Manvel sat on a low stool by the fire, but even as it blazed up he felt a cold wind go through him. He shuddered in spite of himself.

Goat was waiting for him to speak.

"There is one who is a danger to our tribe," Manvel said. "He is bringing in things from the outside that can only destroy our old way of life here on the earth's surface. The gods will surely become angry with us if we do not stop him."

"What are you asking of me?" grunted Goat, who was really pleased to hear there was some danger to the tribe. He had lived on the outside of human so-

ciety for so long that he no longer took any side in
the feuds of the various tribesmen who came to him.
And they did come often—for jealousy in love, for
envy of another man's wealth, for revenge in a
family argument. What matter to him who was right
or wrong. He cared only about the job to be done,
and the payment of chicken, beef and rum he would
get in return.

"Can you . . . can you send an evil wind to this
person?" Manvel was saying.

"To make him die?"

Goat always got right down to the point. He did
not believe in being squeamish about matters of life
and death, since both had lost their value to him.

Manvel opened his mouth to reply, but the words
choked in his throat. He didn't dare say them. So he
merely nodded his head: yes.

"And who is this man you want destroyed?"

When Manvel told him, the witch doctor's mouth
twitched, as if he had tasted something bitter. He
knew well the reputation of Shun's father for being
active in the hamlet, even holding down an important
post in the tribe's ceremonial center the year before.

The gods looked with favor on such people.

"Do you know his animal spirit companion?" Goat asked Manvel.

"No," admitted Manvel. "I have tried to find out, but he has told no one."

"He is a strong man," grunted Goat, spitting into the fire. "He may have a strong jaguar spirit. If so, he might have too much power for my spell."

"And then?"

"Then the sickness could be turned back on me, and I would be the one to die."

"I would reward you well with corn and rum—with anything you wanted," urged Manvel.

"I would want nothing if I were dead," sniggered Goat.

It seemed that Manvel had come in vain.

The two of them sat in darkness in the cave as the fire went down. Outside an owl gave a shrill shriek that made Manvel shiver even more than the cold. He wondered if it were true that witch doctors could control certain birds and summon them as messengers at their will.

Now Goat spoke as if the owl had inspired him.

"This man's soul may be too strong for me to overcome, yes. But what about a child he loves?"

"He has an elder son named Shun of whom he is proud."

"Do you know the boy's animal twin spirit?"

"No. He may not even know it yet himself."

"Well, even if it were a jaguar, it would be a young one, without much power," said Goat, thinking out loud. "There would be no danger to us in sending the spell to him. If anything happens to him, the father will suffer deeply. I have found that a son's death is the cruelest punishment for any man."

"Then do it," cried Manvel, with satisfaction. "That will teach him not to play with the gods— or me."

Now, having accomplished his mission, Manvel rose to leave. He was anxious to get back to his house under the cover of darkness.

"What will you need?" he asked at the door.

"Everything," said Goat. And he named a long list of things ending with rum. "Lots of rum," he stressed. He might have added, "not only for the ceremony, but for myself."

Planting

The next day the village life goes on as usual.

Those who have not finished their spring planting hurry to their fields to finish the job before the summer rains come.

Shun's father has already burned the corn stubbles from last year's crop and turned the soil. He has promised Shun he can help put the seeds in the straight rows, which lay waiting for them.

Together the two of them make holes with a pointed digging stick and drop the seeds in. When the summer rains arrive, the little seedlings will grow tall. Then Shun will help his father weed between them with a metal hoe.

"Grow little corn plants," Shun whispers as he drops the seeds. "Remember you are the sunbeams of the gods."

It is hard work out there in the hot sun, but all of

the villagers are used to it. And they know that if the Earth Lord is good to them, they will have a large pile of corn for the next year's tortillas. And perhaps even some extra to sell at market.

So busy are they, that no one notices that Manvel is not in his field—that his brother-in-law is working in his place there.

No one has seen Manvel, his stole still wrapped around his face, taking a bus to San Cristobal at dawn. And no one observes him come home in the evening with his purchases hidden in cotton sugar bags slung over his shoulder.

Black
Magic

Late that night when the village is quiet, the same dark figure hurries down the unlit paths of the hamlet. It is Manvel carrying candles, chickens, flowers, incense and many flasks of the best rum he can find.

When he arrives at the cave, Goat has already set up the small altar from which he will cast his dark magic.

First Goat takes seven colored candles that attract the attention of the demons. He cuts them in half and holds them upside down. For the Zinacantecs believe that everyone's luck is like a burning candle that is spent during his lifetime.

Goat is trying to cut Shun's luck, yes.

Manvel smiles with satisfaction as he watches the candles burn, even as Shun's life will soon be burn-

ing to an end. Then he creeps out of the cave and hurries home.

Goat sits chanting at the small altar, offering rum to the gods, which he knows, from experience, they cannot resist. Then he gives them white candles, which taste to them like tortillas. Long ago he learned that the gods judge a worthy heart by the offerings that are sent. And he has always been very careful to prepare the very best for them.

When he has filled the gods with enough food and drink, he will try to convince them to let Shun's animal spirit companion out of its corral.

"Eat and drink," he chants, never addressing them by name. He secretly thinks them very foolish to accept offerings from one such as himself. "Fill your sacred stomachs, and then listen to your humble son who would ask you a favor," he keeps repeating.

All that night the loathsome witch doctor chants, drinks rum and offers even more to the trusting gods. Until now they have always granted what he wanted. He is sure that they will tonight.

Shun's candles continue burning lower and lower. His time is running out, yes.

The
Ancestral
Gods

High up on their sacred mountain, in their great
banquet hall, the gods are sitting at their long table
enjoying the offerings of pure rum and white, un-
broken candles that Goat is sending to them. They
always look forward to his feasts, which have a
special tang the other shamans have not mastered.

Like their descendants below, the gods always sit
at table in order of rank—the very oldest first, those
who lived in the ancient times of the Maya, and so
on up through the ages to the present era.

The oldest gods are the smallest, for men were
not as tall long ago as they are now. They wear
fathered hairpieces and garments made from the
quetzl bird. Indeed, so tiny are they, it is hard to see

anything more of them than the tips of their feathered heads bobbing up and down over the table top.

The gods from more recent times are much larger. They wear the red-striped tunics of the people below. They could pass unnoticed among the tribesmen in the hamlet.

But all of them have the same passion as their descendants for rum and tortillas. The more the better.

For hours while Goat chants, the gods sit eating and drinking without stop. As they drink they become so merry they are ready to do anything that Goat asks.

What is Goat saying?

The boy Shun is disrespectful? Will not keep his clothes clean? Will not help his father in the fields? Will not take part in the religious ceremonies of the village? Will not honor the gods?

Yes, he must be punished, this wicked boy!

There is but one thing to do, and they do it. They rise together from their chairs, make their way unsteadily from the banquet hall out to the corrals. There they search about drunkenly in the various pens until they find the young jaguar they are look-ing for.

The little jaguar has been asleep at his mother's side. He does not stir when he hears the gods ap-proaching. Why should he? They have always played with him, yes, embraced him and given him tender care.

And so now he is startled when they rush in, pull him rudely to his feet and shove him out the door of the corral!

Before he understands what is happening, the gate slams shut behind him. He is alone, separated from his mother and all the other jaguars, who do not dare roar out in protest.

He is outside the Supernatural Corral!

The dark woods loom ahead menacingly. One of the assistants of the gods reaches over the fence and prods him with a sharp stick. He has no choice but to move away from the corral, away from his mother, into the unknown jungle.

Unsteadily the little jaguar takes his first uncertain steps toward the forest.

The
Illness

At the same moment the little jaguar is being forced out of the corral, Shun awakens with a strong throbbing in his head and pain in his stomach. He sits up on his mat. But then not wanting to disturb the others, he lays down again and tries to sleep.

He tosses fitfully.

In a dream he sees his jaguar twin stumbling about on the mountainside. He reaches out a hand to help it, to lead it back to the corral, but he cannot grab it. Each time he is about to wrap his arms about it, the jaguar vanishes into the thicket. Shun is left holding thin air.

In his dream Shun runs up and down the mountain path, searching for his lost jaguar. But he can not find it. His twin spirit is beyond his help.

By dawn Shun's body is racked with fever. He is

shaking all over. He cannot lift even his head.

His mother, hearing his moaning, wakes his father. The two of them rub him with salt and talk about what this unexpected illness could be.

"It came on so suddenly," says his mother. "Not like the sickness that took his little brother. That came on slowly and put spots on his face and body."

Shun's mother has not mentioned that lost child since the day she saw his coffin lowered into the ground. But now the fear that her eldest child might die makes the sad memory of that other one return. Shun, after all, is her firstborn, and though she will never admit it, he is the favorite. The one on whom the hopes of the family rest. It is Shun who is to take over his father's fields; Shun who is to tend the house cross when they are gone. Katal and Maruch being girls, will marry into another clan.

"He is not coughing, so it is not the sickness of the lungs that has taken so many children in the past," observes Shun's father. "And even that had warnings. They coughed for many weeks before they went."

"There has been no warning," agrees his mother.

"He was fine in the fields yesterday. He is used to long periods in the sun. There was no wind."

"No warning," repeats his wife. And her husband knows what she means. A spell from a witch doctor can cause illness to come suddenly, mysteriously and even fatally.

"I will get a shaman immediately," cries Shun's father, pulling on his pants and tunic. "The old woman who lives to the north might be the best. She can get here quickly and start what is to be done right away."

"It is said that she cured the baby on the other side of the valley last week when everyone thought it would surely die," says Shun's mother.

"I am going," calls her husband from the door.

"Go," she replies. "I will start making tortillas for a curing ceremony."

And she puts her fingers gently on Shun's fevered head.

"We will help you," she says softly. "Help is coming."

But Shun cannot hear.

Part 3

THE GREAT VISION

The Shaman

The shaman is an old woman dressed in a long black robe with a black shawl over her head. The only spot of color on her is the gold front tooth, which flashes when she talks. It is a sign of some wealth gained from her position over the years.

She is, in fact, the only woman among one hundred shamans in the tribe. When she was young, she dreamed three times that the ancestral gods called her to Senior Great Mountain and trained her in their ways. From that time she has been a shaman and has seen many things that other people cannot see.

Now she walks slowly over to Shun's mat, leaning on the long bamboo staff that is the emblem of her trade. Shun's breathing is coming heavily, as if the passing of each minute makes it more difficult. His sister, Katal, is huddled next to the fire, holding the baby who seems too alarmed by all the commotion to cry.

The old woman puts down her staff and stands over Shun. Picking up his right arm, she feels the pulse in his elbow and then in the wrist. She does the same with his left arm.

She is talking to his blood, *pulsing* him, as it is called, determining the seriousness of his illness. For the People of the Bat believe that blood talks, and a good shaman can understand what it is saying.

Now she must find out if the illness is due to Shun's inner soul having some of its thirteen parts knocked out by the ancestral gods, or to his animal spirit companion having been let out of the Supernatural Corral.

She chants in a high singsong voice as she does this, talking to the blood, coaxing it:

> *Let the blood talk to me,*
> *with one great pulsing,*
> *with one small pulsing,*
> *talk blood smoothly,*

The Shaman

talk as you flow,
talk blood loudly,
Tell me all you know.

The shaman stands there for a long time over Shun. Her eyes are closed, and sometimes she seems to nod in agreement, at other times she seems to nod in her sleep.

Shun's mother and father watch her face, hoping to read on it some of the information she is getting.

Finally she puts Shun's arms down for the last time, opens her eyes and stands up straight.

"The blood tells me it is very serious," she says. "It tells me that the gods have been persuaded by someone to let Shun's twin animal spirit out of its corral."

Shun's mother gives a little cry, but the shaman does not seem to notice.

"The blood tells me his twin is a jaguar, yes. It is in danger in the forest."

"Who would do such a thing!" exclaims Shun's father. And then, as if he knows the answer, he adds, "But why to Shun? Why not to me?"

"We will find out *who* in time," says the shaman. "And why. But now we must act quickly. If anything happens to the jaguar—if it falls over a cliff or gets shot by a hunter, I will have no power to help Shun."

"Tell us what to do," pleads Shun's father desperately. His wife is weeping at his side. Katal is wailing by the fire, and the baby is wailing with her.

"We must prepare as quickly as possible for my most difficult curing ceremony—the Great Vision."

"It will all be done," says Shun's father.

"And what should I do?" asks his mother.

"You must choose four women," the shaman tells her. "One must gather as many red geraniums as she can find. Another must go to the water hole to wash Shun's clothes with soaproot, for the gods love cleanliness. And the other two women must grind the maize for the tortillas. We will need many tortillas."

"It will all be done," says Shun's mother.

They choose Shun's godparents to help them, as well as his uncles and aunts who have come as soon as they heard what is happening.

"What can I do?" asks Romin.

"You can accompany me home for now," says the

shaman, picking up her staff. "I will rest there until all is ready. Then you can come back for me when the ceremony is about to begin."

Romin is a little afraid of the shaman, yes. But he is so eager to help Shun that he does not hesitate to go with her.

Preparations

Shun lies semi-conscious as people come and go performing their various tasks. Sometimes his whole body trembles as if something has seized him. But usually he is quiet, as if he is far away.

Romin is back, and sitting by the bed, brushing away flies and speaking to his friend under his breath.

"Can you hear me, Shun? It is me, Romin. I didn't sell flowers on the road today because you weren't there. I need you, Shun, so please come back to us."

As he speaks, the women are grinding maize by the fire. Some of the dough is mixed with Shun's mother's tears. They are as bitter as the limewater she boils the maize kernels in to soften them before grinding.

Katal is there too, by her side, helping pat the dough into flat pancakes. Until this moment she has only made mud patties in the yard, pressing them, rolling them, pretending they are tortillas. But now her mother says she is old enough to make real ones with her and the other women. Katal is very proud that she is allowed to help make Shun well.

Shun's father has Romin help him make a wood enclosure around Shun's bed. It looks very much like the corral in which the jaguar lived. Later this will be an important part of the ceremony.

Then the two of them set a table running east to west on which they place a package of candles pointing east—the place where Father Sun rises.

All is ready—the food, the clean clothes, the incense, the flowers, the rum.

Romin goes to fetch the shaman, taking with him a bottle of rum and two rolls. He runs along the back paths of the village, feeling very important, as if Shun's life hangs on each step he takes.

He is breathless when he arrives.

She is already waiting for him by her gate.

The
Great
Vision

Before the shaman enters Shun's house, she bows and prays at the house cross just outside. It is the Cross of the Fathers. She is telling his ancestors what is happening, and what she is about to do. She is asking for all the help they can give her.

Now she comes inside and kneels and prays at the long table.

Everyone comes to her, bowing in respect.

She touches them one by one lightly on the forehead with the back of her right hand, thus *releasing* them.

Then she goes to the table and chants a prayer to the gods. She prays not only to the ancestral ones in the mountains, but even to the ones whom the

Spanish Conquistadors brought over when they came hundreds of years ago in their large ships.

Yes, she prays to the foreign gods too—to Jesus Christ, to Mary, to the saints, to all who might listen. For although the People of the Bat have never mixed with the Spaniards, they let their gods mix with those alien ones.

The Mayan gods are generous—they do not mind the Catholic gods sharing the beauty of their land. They do not mind the Catholic churches next to their own ancestral crosses in the hamlets. They do not mind because they know that they are still the main gods in the hearts of their people.

While the shaman is calling to all the various gods and saints, it is Romin's job to pour rum for her. Then he pours it for all the men in order of their age and rank, and after that, for the women.

Romin goes from one to the other with a tiny shot glass, waits as each bows to the shaman, gulps it down and hands it back to him to be filled for the next person. He even takes a swig himself when it is his turn at the end.

He feels he needs it.

Just when Romin is sure he is going to keel over from too much rum, the shaman asks for a large pot. Into it she places the water of the seven sacred water holes, along with some of the plants that have been gathered in the mountains. Then she puts it on the fire to heat.

While she is waiting for it to boil, she prays over the candles. The words she speaks will reach the ancestral gods as she utters them.

At the same time, the gods will be receiving her offerings at their great banquet hall—the candles, tortillas and the rum.

As she presents the candles, which she knows are their favorite kind, she chants in a different voice, as if it is Shun who is speaking:

> *See how I suffer,*
> *I, so young and innocent,*
> > *Your son,*
> > *Your flower,*
> > *Your sprout.*
> *Help me in my pain,*
> *Help me with your pardon,*

Your son,
Your flower,
Your sprout,
    Who is suffering,
    Who is miserable.

It seems that while the shaman is praying, a soft breeze blows over the little jaguar as he stumbles along in the forest.

He has not known where to go since he left the Supernatural Corral.

He is afraid to go down the path, but he is also afraid here in the dense thicket.

Yet this strong spirit knows that he cannot be afraid. It is as if something is telling him he is a jaguar, the most powerful cat in the jungle, from whom all other creatures move in fear and respect.

It is as if the soft breeze is blowing fear away from him for that moment. He moves courageously through the unknown terrain. The yellow coloring of his skin, the dark spots on his pelt, blend in with nature's own designs on tree and leaf and stone.

Still he is just a young jaguar. When he hears a

strange noise, he freezes. When he is startled by the sudden movement of a branch nearby, he begins to run and cannot stop until he is overcome by exhaustion.

When he is tired, he just lies down where he is, panting, gulping for air, his throat choking, his thick chest heaving, his lean body flattened as if he might never rise again.

The birds overhead know the jaguar. They know he will rise again.

His body is bleeding where sharp thorns have scratched it.

His paw throbs from stumbling over a jagged rock.

Never has he been alone like this, unattended. Always there have been assistants to the gods embracing him, brushing him, feeding him, loving him. He does not know the way of the wild, this tame and sheltered animal spirit. It is as if he is being tested for something—but for what? Or as if he is being punished—but for what?

He knows that he is innocent.

The birds overhead know that he is innocent. But

they know that will not help him now.

The little jaguar thinks of the young boy who came to visit him in the corral—his twin. At the thought of Shun, he feels strong again. He manages to rise to his feet once more. Maybe he can go to him for help.

He takes a few steps, but he can find no scent of Shun on the wind.

He begins to run again, searching for his twin spirit.

For hours he circles around, frantically. Wild boar and deer jump out of his way. Squirrels and rabbits scatter. Toucans and parrots flap their colorful wings. But he does not notice any of them.

He is hot, he is thirsty, he is hungry. He is lost.

The birds overhead know that he is in serious trouble—even if he is a jaguar.

On the earth's surface, the shaman takes the water from the fire and brings it over to Shun's bed. The laurel and myrtle plants in it will strengthen him.

With a large clean cloth she gently bathes his body.

Shun stirs slightly, as he feels the warm moisture sink into his dry skin.

But he does not open his eyes.

It is just enough to feel it. It is said that heat is healing.

As the shaman continues to bathe Shun, a warm rain comes down from the skies over the little jaguar.

He stands there, letting it run over his body.

He opens his mouth and lets some of it drop into his parched throat.

It feels so good. It is cleansing something very sore inside him. And outside, too, for it soothes the scratches. It soothes his paw.

The rain gives him fresh energy, yes.

He starts to move in a kind of trot, a purposeful movement through the jungle, although he still does not know where he is going.

The birds overhead do not know either.

The shaman has put clean clothes on Shun. They smell of incense.

Now she grabs one of the black chickens and

bathes it in the same water she used for Shun. Then she takes a needle and punctures the chicken's neck, letting the blood drip out into a cup.

She holds Shun's head up and forces the blood into his mouth, down his throat.

As the blood trickles into Shun's body, the jaguar feels its blood running stronger, too.

He trots faster now. He is dashing through the jungle.

The monkeys stop chattering in the trees as he crashes by.

All of the forest is watching, listening.

The birds follow him overhead. They know he is running toward a cliff—toward the dreaded precipice. More than one animal spirit has disappeared over it.

They know that if he does not see it in time, he too will disappear.

The shaman is sewing the chicken's neck back up. She places the body on a plate of pine needles.

Soon she will go to a mountaintop and leave this

black chicken under a cross for the Mayan gods. She hopes they will accept it in place of Shun's soul.

For the time has come in the Great Vision curing ceremony when the shaman, together with the patient and his family, are to take a trip to all the sacred spots on the nearby mountains.

Shun's mother has been wondering how her son can possibly make the journey. Even if he were to be carried on his father's back, it would be too strenuous for him.

The shaman has already thought of this.

"I will take a piece of Shun's clothing with me, in his place," she says. "His tunic. It will represent him on the trip. The gods will not mind."

And so everyone makes ready to leave. The travelling basket is packed with candles and red geraniums, pine needles and boughs to be offered to the mountain gods. There is even chicken and rum for the people to have on the journey.

The shaman is careful to leave one bottle of rum on the table. She wants to keep the communication between the house and the gods open, while she is gone.

Then with only Shun's mother and the two little ones remaining behind, the party starts off.

Katal waves to them as they go.

Romin carries the candles, and the men the heavy baskets.

The shaman walks at the very end of the line, which is considered the place of honor.

Shun's Third Dream

While the shaman is praying for him in the mountain, Shun has a frightening dream.

He sees his jaguar wandering blindly toward the edge of the cliff. The jaguar does not know the drop is there. He is almost to it.

"Stop!" Shun tries to call to him. "There is danger!"

But the jaguar cannot hear him.

The jaguar has reached the cliff now. His left front leg slips over the ledge.

"Stop!" Shun is screaming. "Stop!"

As if he hears Shun's warning at last, the jaguar tries to pull back. For a moment it seems he will not succeed, that he will lose his balance and fall.

But with all of his mighty jaguar strength, he manages to get his leg back over the top of the cliff and drag his whole body away from it.

His heart is pounding so loudly that Shun can actually hear it.

The jaguar's heart and Shun's heart beat together like one great drum in the void.

The jaguar finds a cave nearby and creeps into it.

He sleeps, even as Shun sleeps, both of them breathing together.

But they are not out of danger—either of them.

The jaguar knows instinctively that he must not stay too long in one spot. One part of him does not sleep, but is watching for it knows not what. Now he gets up and moves on his dazed, weary way.

"Find your way back to the corral," Shun is mumbling in his sleep.

"What are you saying?" his mother asks. "Tell me, Shun, and I will do it for you, anything you want."

But Shun is silent again. He knows that this is one time his mother is powerless to help him. And he must not interrupt his dream.

For now he sees a dark figure making its way up

the mountain path. It is carrying a gun, looking for an animal. It is a hunter.

If only his jaguar can smell his scent and escape him!

But the hunter is too smart. He is walking in a direction where the wind cannot get his smell and carry it to the animal.

The hunter walks along with confidence. He knows now for sure that some creature is loose from the corral. He hears the sound of its tired body dragging through the thicket.

The hunter begins to stalk the jaguar.

Dawn

The shaman and the group are back from their pilgrimage to the mountains.

The shaman is washing Shun's hands and feet with the same water she used for his bath earlier. She adds more pine boughs and flowers to the fencing around him, as if she is preparing for a festival.

Shun wants to tell her that the hunter is out there on Senior Great Mountain. That he has spotted the jaguar and is lifting his gun. The jaguar has just seen him, but his body is paralyzed with fear. He cannot move.

"Save my jaguar," Shun tries to cry out. His lips open, but no words come.

The shaman seems to sense what he is saying, yes.

She quickly kills the second black chicken and throws it onto his body.

Everyone watches closely. They know that if the

chicken jumps around a lot while dying, Shun will improve.

"The chicken is dancing!" Romin shrieks excitedly.

"He is dancing, dancing!" repeats Katal.

The chicken does seem to be dancing in its death throes, yes. It falls in a wilted heap onto Shun, with its head to the east.

"It's a good sign," says the shaman, satisfied that the chicken has behaved properly at this crucial moment.

She hangs the dead chicken over Shun's bed until he can eat it.

Up on the mountain, as if dancing with the chicken, the jaguar begins to move. He springs with a graceful leap back into the underbrush, taking the hunter by surprise.

But the hunter soon realizes what is happening, and bounds in after him.

Everyone in Shun's house is smiling now, except the shaman.

She seems to know that things are not going right just yet, in spite of all she has done. The gods, still full from Goat's banquet, have not touched her offerings on their table.

There is little time to lose now.

The shaman lights more candles and more—this time tallow ones, which are as meat to the gods.

She urges everyone in the house to drink even more rum, although they are already swaying from the effects of what they have had. The gods can hear you better when you are filled with rum.

Romin opens bottle after bottle.

As he pours for each person, he gives his own special prayer to the gods:

> *Please listen, holy fathers,*
> *Hear me, holy mothers,*
> *I am only a young boy,*
> *A humble piece of earth,*
> *But my friend Shun,*
> > *Is your son,*
> > *Your flower,*
> > *Your joy.*

Dawn

Stand up for him,
Stand firm beside him,
Beside your humble boy,
  Your son,
  Your flower,
  Your joy.

The Banquet Hall of the Gods

The ancestral gods are sitting at their long banquet table snoozing from all the food and rum that Goat has sent them.

They do not even see all the delicacies that Shun's shaman has sent up.

Who can say what makes them stir—whether it is Romin's earnest words or the shaman's or the scent of the freshly killed black chicken, or the aroma of the newly opened bottles of rum?

Suddenly their noses begin to twitch, one even sneezes. Their mouths open and close as if they are dreaming of chewing something.

It seems impossible that the gods, all bloated as they are, can be tempted to eat and drink more. But

then gods can do anything. That's why they are gods.

One by one, from the most ancient on up the table, they raise their glasses and drink the new rum. At first just a few sips, and then more and more.

It wakes them up, stimulates their appetites.

They taste the tortilla-candles. Then the candles that are as meat. Delicious!

It is as if the food has opened their ears. Now they hear Romin's and the shaman's voices clearly. They hear the father and the mother, too, and the aunts and uncles and friends. They hear such a babble of voices it seems that everyone is speaking at once.

What news is this from the earth's surface?

A boy has been falsely accused!

His little jaguar has been let out of its corral!

Is it possible?

They try a little more rum to convince themselves they are hearing correctly. A few more tortillas, too.

They decide it is not only possible, it is true!

An innocent boy, and in clean clothing, too!

The gods rise together from their long banquet table, all sizes and shapes of them from the beginning of time, and run out to the jaguar stalls.

They are still clutching their tortillas in their hands, eating on the way.

The little jaguar is not in his corral. His mother is lying there alone, looking up at them sadly.

They call to their assistants: "Find the little jaguar!"

Gods and assistants run about in all directions through the jungle.

Where can he be?

Is it too late?

Has he been shot by a hunter?

If so, the gods can do nothing.

Meanwhile, down on earth's surface, Shun is being lifted from his bed with the fence around it, and then placed back into it, as if he is being put into a corral.

The shaman is showing the gods how the little jaguar must be safely returned to his pen.

The gods and assistants are still scurrying about the mountain looking everywhere for the little jaguar.

Now they see him. He is racing desperately toward them.

But who is that pursuing him? A hunter!

The hunter does not see the gods. He just sees the jaguar. He raises his gun to shoot. The gun is high, his finger on the trigger.

The gods raise their hands in unison.

The hunter's arm is frozen. He cannot move it, not even his finger. He stands there watching dumbly as the gods lead the little jaguar back to the corral.

The jaguar's mother jumps up when she sees him coming in. She bounds over to him, licks him all over just as the shaman had cleaned Shun.

The little jaguar falls into an exhausted heap at her side.

The hunter slips away into the night.

The gods return to the banquet table where they continue eating and drinking until they fall once more into a stuporous condition, their chins on their plates.

The Cure

Shun is sleeping easily now, just like his jaguar. His fever is gone. He is breathing regularly. Finally he opens his eyes.

He says his first words: "I am hungry."

The shaman cuts up the black chicken for him. He must eat this to get his strength.

"The gods have heard us," the shaman says. Her voice is thick from too much rum, too much food, too little sleep. But it is jubilant.

"Your jaguar is back in its corral," she informs Shun. "You will get well."

Then she picks up her staff and walks unsteadily to the door.

Romin and some of the men stagger after her with baskets of presents—tortillas, chicken and rum.

Just as Shun is waking up, everyone else is about to collapse.

Recuperation

For the next two weeks Shun has to stay in bed. And even after that he must remain in the house until the shaman is satisfied that he is safe leaving it.

The shaman has left definite instructions for the things Shun may or may not do:

HE MAY NOT EAT CABBAGE OR BEANS.

HE MAY NOT BE LEFT ALONE.

HE MAY NOT TALK TO ANYONE.

HE MAY NOT HAVE VISITORS.

For it is believed that during this period the ancestral gods come regularly to visit the patient, and see how he is getting along.

If the ancestors are present, Shun does not notice them.

He lies for hours on his back watching the shadows that the flickering fire throws on the adobe walls.

He thinks of his jaguar lying quietly in its corral, also getting back his strength. Since the fencing around his bed is still up, it is as if he too is in the corral.

When he dreams at night, he and the jaguar are lying together, side by side, their bodies touching, as if they are one.

After two weeks the shaman comes and takes down the fencing around Shun's bed. She bathes him again, rubs him with flowers, prays for him and buries the chicken bones behind the house cross.

But Shun must still wait three days before he can get up.

Now he lies on his side for hours watching his mother weave outside the doorway.

She uses only black wool, since white might attract blows from the demons. Everyone knows what they feel like, yes. Suddenly, for no reason, you have a sharp pain. And you realize the demons have whacked you.

He watches his sister, Katal, weaving on her small toy loom, imitating her mother.

He watches the baby Maruch crawling around on

the ground, trying to grab at the wool.

He watches his father, at night by the fire, watching him.

Now there is but one more thing Shun must do to be considered completely well. He must take a series of three baths in the little shed attached to his home, which his people call the sweat house. It is like a sauna—burning pieces of oak wood are placed over lava rocks and then removed, leaving only coals and hot rocks. Water is then sprinkled on the rocks to make them steam.

It feels good. Shun fans the air with a palm leaf to circulate it. Then he lies down with his feet towards the rocks for fifteen minutes.

High in the Supernatural Corral, the jaguar is lying stretched out in the sun. He feels the hot rays go through him, purifying him, giving him strength.

He feels the love of the gods and of Shun.

After his third bath, the shaman declares Shun completely cured.

He is allowed to work in his flower garden.

The shaman's powers have worked well, yes. She has not only cured Shun, but she has managed to return the sickness to the sender—in this case back to both Goat and Manvel.

It happened like this—one night she burned seven candles of different colors while asking the gods to close the eyes of those who had caused trouble for the patient.

And the gods agreed.

Romin brought the news the next morning. "Manvel is seriously ill. Only the most expensive curing ceremonies can save him. And Goat is said to be so sick in his cave that his groans were heard coming over the hills."

It was true.

When Manvel did rise from his bed again, he said nothing about the electric lines, which by then had been installed in the hamlet.

In fact, he went out of his way to avoid all of Shun's family.

As for Goat, it was rumored that he had disappeared from his cave. No one could say if he were dead or alive.

The
Future

It is just before dawn of the morning that Shun is allowed to go back up on the road to sell flowers.

His soul is out visiting in a dream again.

It is so powerful that he wakes his family. They cannot understand it. But they know he has dreamed something special, yes.

They quickly call the shaman, and he repeats it to her.

"I dreamed," said Shun, "that once again I had climbed the path to the Supernatural Corral. But this time I was met by one of the assistants and invited to come into the house of the oldest of the ancestral gods. I found him sitting in his feathers at a long table with all the shamans of our tribe there, including you."

The shaman smiles mysteriously.

"I bowed to all present," continues Shun, "and kneeled at the west end of the table."

"And then?" asks the shaman.

"And then the oldest god asked me if I was prepared to become a shaman. I wasn't sure I was, but I said 'yes.' So he gave me all types of candles and flowers I would need for a curing ceremony. And he taught me how to say the proper prayers."

"And then?" prods the shaman.

"And then he gave me a black robe to wear and had me kneel while he made the sign of the cross on my forehead. As I stood up, a very sick baby about Maruch's age was brought in. He asked me what was wrong with her."

"Did you know?" asks the shaman, who is clearly very much involved with Shun's dream.

"Yes, I saw at once that she had lost some pieces of her soul. So I lit some candles, said a prayer and hit the ground with an oak branch while shouting: 'Come, come!' And it worked. All the parts of the soul returned at my bidding to the body of the baby. She was cured."

Shun pauses. "And then I woke up."

The shaman says nothing now, as if she is still in the dream.

"What does it mean?" asks Shun. "It was so strange, and yet I knew just what to do."

"You have just had a curing dream," says the shaman. "The gods have sent you their first call to become a curer like myself."

"But why?" asks Shun.

"Those who see, dream well," says the old woman. "The gods must believe that you are one who truly sees."

"Did you have such a dream once?" asks Shun.

"Of course. Those whom the gods have chosen to become shamans have three dreams in which they are called up to Senior Great Mountain to perform cures. You have just had your first."

"When will he have his second?" asks Shun's mother.

"In another year, perhaps. And the last one a year after that."

They all thought about this in silence.

"And when the dreams come, Shun, you must not refuse the god's call. To do so, is to die."

"I would not refuse!" exclaims Shun.

"I know you wouldn't," says the shaman, her smile still mysterious, her gold tooth flashing. "And I know you will be a good shaman, and work only for the well-being of your people."

Shun says nothing about his dream to Romin but he thinks about it as they sell their flowers.

And he is still thinking about it later that day as they wander through the hamlet watching their tribesmen install electric bulbs hung on long cords in their various houses. At night the lights gleam through the doorways like so many stars lighting the courtyards.

No demon would dare come near their houses now. No witch would dare lurk outside the doors. No ball of fire would dare bounce around in the fields.

Shun thinks about his dream so much in the next few weeks that sometimes it seems he is in a dream from which he never wakes.

"Here comes a car!" Romin calls to him more than once from his spot farther down the road.

On one such day, as he is standing there, a familiar car comes by from San Cristobal. It stops on the other side of the road and out of it steps the very boy with pale blue eyes that he had seen arriving so long ago.

How long ago he cannot even think now with all that has happened.

The boy holds out his hand with a few pesos and

smiles as Shun hands him the flowers. They cannot speak to each other, except with their eyes.

Shun is aware that he is smiling back at the boy, something he would never have done before. He is aware that he is being friendly.

Shun watches as the boy returns to the car, and it continues on its way down the mountain towards the lowlands and on into central Mexico.

Shun knows that someday he will have enough Spanish to speak to that boy, should he ever return again. He sees himself studying from his school books under the light bulb his father has hung near the fire.

He sees the future, yes.

He sees himself going to the market in San Cristobal to buy the things he will need for his curing ceremonies.

He sees himself with his shaman's bamboo staff going off to help sick people.

On the earth's surface and in his dreams, he sees himself growing, stretching and reaching out, just as the highway does beyond the lowlands into the unknown.

And he sees his jaguar growing with him, grow-

ing strong and firm in his body and spirit, ready. to accompany him on all the adventures of his life.

He sees well, yes.